PUFFIN BOOKS

DIZ AND THE BIG
AND OTHER STORIE

Meet a host of amusing characters in these three
light-hearted stories from three top authors. First
meet Diz and her dog Digger who are having a
serious spring-clean when they find a fat burglar
fast asleep in the corner. Diz goes down to the
police station to report him, but meanwhile the
burglar has been busy. Indeed so busy, that Diz
doesn't want her burglar to go to prison after all –
but Sergeant Scoop is expected any minute!

The next story, *The Day the Smells Went Wrong*,
is a good and smelly mystery involving Jackie and
Phil, who put clothes pegs on their noses and try
to help the Chief Inspector of Smells solve the
riddle of the mixed-up smells.

Finally, in our third story meet the lovable Mr
String who thinks his dream has come true when
he is asked to perform his 'Rocket Concerto' at a
concert at the Royal Albert Hall. On the big night
the Hall doesn't look quite like he was expecting,
but after all that practising Mr String is
determined to carry on.

Diz and the Big Fat Burglar

and Other Stories

**Jolyne Knox, Catherine Sefton
and Margaret Stuart Barry**

**Illustrated by
Paula Martyr**

PUFFIN BOOKS

PUFFIN BOOKS

Published by the Penguin Group
Penguin Books Ltd, 27 Wrights Lane, London W8 5TZ,
England
Penguin Books USA Inc., 375 Hudson Street, New York, New
York 10014, USA
Penguin Books Australia Ltd, Ringwood, Victoria, Australia
Penguin Books Canada Ltd, 10 Alcorn Avenue, Toronto,
Ontario, Canada M4V 3B2
Penguin Books (NZ) Ltd, 182–190 Wairau Road, Auckland 10,
New Zealand

Penguin Books Ltd, Registered Offices: Harmondsworth,
Middlesex, England

First published separately by Hamish Hamilton Children's
Books: *Diz and the Big Fat Burglar*, 1987; *The Day the
Smells Went Wrong* and *Mr String*, 1988
Published in Puffin Books 1991
10 9 8 7 6 5 4 3 2

Text copyright © Margaret Stuart Barry (*Diz and the Big
Fat Burglar*), 1987; Catherine Sefton (*The Day the Smells
Went Wrong*), 1988; Jolyne Knox (*Mr String*), 1988
Illustrations copyright © Paula Martyr, 1991
All rights reserved

Filmset in Monophoto Century Schoolbook

Printed in England by Clays Ltd, St Ives plc

Contents

For
Nick Bate

Diz and the Big Fat Burglar

Margaret Stuart Barry

Diz was a small girl aged six and a half. She lived with her dog, Digger, in a VERY messy house.

'Just look at my corner!' Digger growled. 'I can't find my rubber bone.'

The postman was cross too. He had to climb up a ladder and post the letters through the bedroom window.

'All right,' Diz sighed. 'I suppose we'd better tidy up.'

Digger was pleased. He rushed around, wagging his tail and barking a song he knew about spring cleaning.

Diz put on a bright pair of overalls, and found a fluffy feather duster.

Digger fetched a shovel and a sweeping brush.

They started to tidy Digger's corner first.

They found a cricket bat, a pink bear with one eye missing, a cracked teapot, a mouse, a broken doll, Digger's rubber

bone and – a BIG FAT
BURGLAR who was fast asleep.

Diz and Digger tidied up the
good things and threw away the
broken ones. But they didn't
know what to do with the
burglar.

'We can't very well tidy HIM
up,' said Digger.

'And we can't very well throw him away,' said Diz.

They sat down for a rest and a think, and stared at the burglar.

'Give him a dust,' said Digger.

So Diz tickled him with her feather duster.

The burglar woke up, and
sneezed very loudly.

'You're a BURGLAR!' Diz
said.

The burglar looked down at his
stripy jumper and sackful of
stolen things.

'So I am!' he said, and fell asleep again.

Diz and Digger went to see Sergeant Scoop at the Police Station.

'We have a big fat burglar in our house. Please would you come and collect him at once,' Diz said.

'Certainly,' said Sergeant Scoop, who didn't believe Diz one little bit. 'I'll come along when I've finished my dinner.'

Sergeant Scoop went and told the Chief Inspector that there was a silly little kid, with a silly little dog, who had a dangerous criminal in their house.

'Gosh!' yawned the Chief Inspector.

When Diz and Digger got home, they found the burglar had been busy. He had finished tidying Digger's corner. He had done all the washing-up, and had made some delicious scones.

Diz and Digger felt guilty.

Just before bedtime, the burglar filled all the hot-water bottles and set the table for morning.

'I wonder why Sergeant Scoop hasn't come?' whispered Digger.

'Perhaps he has more important criminals to catch,' said Diz, hopefully.

Next day, the burglar said,

'Oh gosh! I seem to have your clock in my sack. It must have dropped in by mistake.'

And he put it back on the mantelpiece.

Then the burglar went out into
the garden and dug it all over.
He planted peas and beans,
carrots and onions.

That evening he knitted a
bright red cardigan for Diz, and
a woolly hat with ear-flaps for
Digger.

The more good things the big
fat burglar did, the more Diz and
Digger wished they hadn't
reported him to Sergeant Scoop.

'Oh gosh!' said the burglar,
'I've found your valuable pot. It
must have fallen into my sack.'

And he put it back on the table.

There was still no sign of
Sergeant Scoop. He was playing
Snap with the Chief Inspector.
Sergeant Scoop was cheating.

Diz and Digger were pleased.
They didn't want the big fat
burglar to go to prison after all.
They decided they should take
him back to his own house where
he would be safe.

'Get all your stuff together,'
Diz told him.

Digger wagged his tail at the
thought of a walk.

The burglar led the way back to his house. It was next door to the Police Station.

Diz knocked on the door. 'We've brought your husband back,' she said.

'Oh, thanks,' said Mrs Burglar, setting out three more silver cups.

'I think your husband should stop stealing,' said Diz.

Mrs Burglar looked astonished, and so did all the little Burglar children.

'But he's always been a
burglar!' she cried. 'And a good
one, too.'

Then all the little Burglar
children began to cry loudly.

'There's a terrible noise going
on in the house next door,

Sergeant Scoop,' complained the
Chief Inspector. 'You'd better go
and see what's happening.
Perhaps they've got a burglar.'
   'Hullo, hullo, hullo,' said
Sergeant Scoop as he went into
the big fat burglar's sitting-room.

'Is everything all right?'

Sergeant Scoop didn't notice the silver football cups, or the twenty television sets, or the golden spoons, or the famous paintings on the walls, or the fifty electric toasters.

'Everything's fine,' said the burglar.

Sergeant Scoop went back to the Police Station. 'They are having a tea party, I think. That silly little girl and her silly little dog are there too.'

'SNAP!' said the Chief Inspector, who had also been cheating.

Meanwhile, Diz had thought of a brilliant idea.

'My house is FULL of things,' she said. 'Anything you need,

just come and ask me. Then you won't need to steal!'

So whenever the Burglar family wanted something, they asked Diz. And that way, the big fat burglar stayed out of prison, and Diz's house stayed nice and tidy – and so did Digger's corner!

The Day the
Smells Went
Wrong

Catherine Sefton

Jackie and Phil had buttered toast for breakfast.

'Mum?' said Phil. 'This toast smells of tar.'

'Just eat it!' said Mum, who was flying round collecting baby bits and pushchairs and had no time to talk.

'We don't want to,' said Jackie and Phil.

Mum was annoyed, but she hadn't time to fight about it.

'All right,' she said. 'Leave it.'

They piled out of the house in a scurry of schoolbags and pushchairs, and then they had to single file down the pavement outside, where the men were putting fresh tar on the road.

sniff

Sniff went Jackie.

Sniff-sniff went Phil.

'That tar smells of toast!' said Phil.

'And our toast smelt of tar!' said Jackie.

'Oh!' said Somebody.

'Did you say "Oh"?' said Phil to Jackie.

'No, you did!' said Jackie.

They went past the Fruit Shop.

Sniff went Jackie.

Sniff-sniff went Phil.

'Mum, that fruit shop smells of fi . . .' began Jackie, but Mum grabbed her arm. They hustled around the corner, past the Fish Shop.

Sniff went Jackie.

Sniff-sniff went Phil.

The Fish Shop smelt of apples and oranges and tomatoes and grapes.

'Oh NO!' said Somebody.

Phil and Jackie looked around, but there was nobody to be seen.

'In you go!' said Mum. 'See you this afternoon!' and she pushed Phil and Jackie through the school gates, and swerved off down the pavement doing fifty miles an hour with the pushchair.

'Everything smells wrong this morning!' said Phil, when they got inside the school. 'Like this corridor.'

Sniff went Jackie.

Sniff-sniff went Phil.

'It ought to smell of polish and chalk,' said Phil. 'But it doesn't! It smells like . . .'

'. . . like the swimming-pool!' said Jackie.

They both held their noses, and carried on down to Miss Boot's classroom.

Behind them in the corridor, Somebody said: 'Oh! No! O-O-H!'

But nobody heard. Everybody was too busy sniffing and getting confused.

Mr Swift's bicycle smelt of roses and Miss Boot's roses in the classroom smelt of bicycle oil. Miss Boot had put on her new perfume because she was in love with Mr Swift. She wanted him to think she smelt lovely.

'What's that awful cabbage smell, Miss Boot?' Mr Swift said when he met her in the corridor. 'Is it our school dinner?'

And poor Miss Boot cried.

'Oh, OOH!' said Somebody.

Things got worse by breaktime.

Down the corridor, in Miss Boot's room, everything smelt wrong.

Smoky bacon crisps smelt of cornflakes.

Chocolate smelt of carrots.

The teachers' *coffee* smelt of *tea*, and their *tea* smelt of *coffee*, so nobody drank any of it.

And the chalk box smelt of dead dragons with dirty socks!

'OOOOOH! NOOOOO!' said Somebody. 'I'll lose my job!'

'Every time we sniff something that smells wrong, somebody goes "Oh" or "Oh no" or says "I'll lose my job!",' said Jackie.

'It's only me,' said the Somebody, sounding very sad.

Jackie and Phil whirled round. There, sitting on top of the Games Box, was the Somebody.

'Sorry,' he said. 'It's all my fault!'

'Who are you?' said Phil.

'I'm the Chief Inspector of Smells!' said the Somebody. 'I fix the smells when they go wrong.'

'Do it then!' said Phil and Jackie.

'Can't!' said the Chief Inspector of Smells. 'I've lost my Smelling List.'

'*Spelling* List?' said Phil.

'SMELLING List,' said the Chief Inspector of Smells. 'My List of Smells. The smells round here have got all muddled up and I can't put them right without it.'

'Where did you lose it?' said Phil.

'Somewhere in this school!'
said the Chief Inspector.

'Hunt the Smelling List!' said
Jackie.

And Jackie and Phil and the
Chief Inspector of Smells dashed
about looking for the Smelling
List, but they had to stop when
the bell went.

They still hadn't found it by
lunch-break, and then things got
worse.

Nobody wanted to eat mince
meat and cabbage with savoury
sauce that smelt like Miss Boot's
perfume.

'We won't eat that!' all the
children cried.

'Quite right, children,' said Miss Boot, and she scolded the cook.

'We want our dinners!' shouted all the children who took dinners, and they marched around the school waving banners and flags.

'There's nothing else for it,' said Miss Boot. 'Clothes pegs on our noses!'

'Miss, Miss!' said Jackie. 'We can't do lessons with clothes pegs on our noses!'

'Right, Jackie,' said Miss Boot. 'I will send for the parents to

take you home. We cannot teach
with clothes pegs on our noses
either.'

'No work with pegs on!'
cheered all the children.

'Oh yes, there will be!' said
Miss Boot, and she dashed back
to the Staff Room, and came back
with an armful of Spelling Lists.

'One each to everyone in your
class,' she told Phil, and she gave
him a pile.

Phil started giving the
Spelling Lists out. They were like
this:

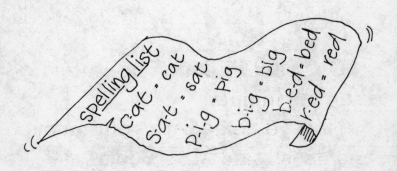

Spelling List
cat = cat
sat = sat
pig = pig
big = big
bed = bed
red = red

But one wasn't. It was like
this:

smelling list
toast = nice
and tasty
tar = hot and
smelly
fish = wet
and salty
fruit = fresh
and sweet

'Oh!' said Phil, and he stuffed
it up his jumper.

'Now go home with your mums
and dads!' said Miss Boot.

They all went home, with pegs
on their noses. Most of the mums
and dads had pegs on their noses
too, because there were odd
smells about.

Meanwhile, back at the school,

the Chief Inspector of Smells was
hard at work on the Smelling
List Phil had slipped to him.

Soon, chocolate smelt like
chocolate and bacon smelt like
bacon and bicycles smelt like

bicycles and Miss Boot smelt like
lavender, which is sweet. She
smelt so sweet that Mr Swift
married her, almost at once.

By the next morning,
everything was all right.

Phil and Jackie came down for breakfast as usual.

'Toast!' said Mum, putting it down on the table.

Sniff went Jackie.

Sniff-sniff went Phil.

And they ate it all up, and had two rounds more, because it smelt so fresh, and buttery, and lovely!

Mr String

Jolyne Knox

Mr Samuel String was a merry
musicmaker. Every day he played
very loud and very fast on his
old violin. He was a clever
musician, but he was very short-
sighted and very forgetful. He
was always getting into dreadful
muddles.

Mr String lodged in a ramshackle old house. His proud landlady, Mrs Miranda Muskett, tried hard to keep 'her Maestro' ship-shape.

One morning an important-looking letter arrived. Mr String opened it curiously.

'Oooh, my goodness me!' he cried. 'For the very first time I am invited to play at the Royal Albert Hall. What a thrill! My "Rocket Concerto" will sound good there.'

He tied another knot in his handkerchief and rushed to invite Mrs Muskett to come too.

As the weeks before the concert went by, Mr String lived in a hubbub of music. Every day the house quaked as he practised

furiously to prepare for the big
night. Mrs Muskett tried in vain
to keep order.

At last the great day came. Mr
String awoke early and plunged
into his bath. He sang at the top

of his voice as he thought of the
marvellous time he would have
playing at the Royal Albert Hall.
He would be like all the famous
musicians – with calls for ten
encores perhaps . . .!

All day long the house was in a turmoil. Mrs Muskett busily cheered up the dusty String concert suit with a stiff brush and a hot iron. She made tasty sandwiches to keep the Maestro's strength up. Meanwhile, Mr String bounced wild notes from the walls and lampshades as his bow flew across the strings.

By the time the cuckoo on the wall wheezed five o'clock, the practising, pressing and polishing were done. Mrs Muskett prepared an early supper of buttered toast with a tasty kipper. Afterwards, Mr String dozed dreamily in front of the hot coals.

Then it was time to leave. He

thanked Mrs Muskett for all her help and said, 'I am most honoured, dear lady, that you will be coming to share the fun.'

He gave a little bow and hurried off to catch his bus.

Mrs Muskett smiled proudly and went to fix her best hat. She wanted to be properly dressed for this important occasion.

At the bus stop, Mr String beamed and bid everyone 'Good day'. There was a muffled mutter from the queue.

'Deary me, this won't do,' he thought. 'I'll give them a cheery tune or two.'

Strangely they seemed glad when the bus came!

The conductor wagged his

finger and said, 'All weapons at the back of the bus, Maestro.'

'Cheeky fellow,' said Mr String to himself.

The bus crawled along. Mr String felt he would never get to the hall on time. But at last he arrived. He walked a short way, then suddenly – there it was – THE ROYAL ALBERT HALL!

Mr String gazed in awe. It seemed even more splendid than he had expected.

'Oh, gosh,' he thought, 'what an evening this will be.'

Tingling nervously, he went to find the artists' entrance.

At the back of the building a few people were waiting to see the performers arrive.

'Odd-looking music lovers,' thought Mr String, feeling uneasy.

The doorman said, 'Evening sport, which one are you, The Grappling Gorilla or Musclecrush Lou?'

Mr String was startled but he went inside boldly.

Suddenly, a big man in a vest appeared.

'Want a rub down, matey?' he grinned.

Mr String jumped. 'Thank you,' he said, trying to look dignified, 'that will not be necessary.'

Shaking nervously, he went into the dressing room and unpacked his violin.

Then, before he knew what had happened, he was whisked towards a door marked 'Arena'. From behind the door there came a loud roaring noise.

'Oh deary, deary me,' worried Mr String, now very alarmed.

In a moment he was through the door. The noise nearly blew him over. High in a roped ring stood the most ferocious man he had ever seen. The Grappling Gorilla flexed his muscles. 'Come on up, Maestro,' he roared.

Inside Mr String's head a small doubt was growing into a very big one. He had muddled something REALLY important this time. What day was his concert anyway?

Before he could blink, Mr String was gripped by The Gorilla.

'Oh, deary me!' he gasped as
he was whirled around. He
struck the strings in a fury of
sparks. The Gorilla winced. On
they spun, getting giddier and
dizzier. Notes flashed all around.
The Gorilla puffed and grunted.

Suddenly, after a specially
shattering scale, The Gorilla

wilted. He clapped his hands to his ears.

'Cor,' he groaned, 'this is deadly, mate. Let me out of 'ere!'

Amidst the uproar, Mr String was named the victor. Amazed, he grinned bashfully with relief.

The crowd cheered wildly. Musclecrush Lou, who had arrived late, gaped with astonishment as Mr String was given the shining, silver cup. He was the hero of the night.

'Now then, give my Maestro some room!' ordered Mrs Muskett, bustling through. 'My stars, Maestro,' she said, dusting Mr String down, 'a proper pickle you've got yourself into this time. Who'd ever 'ave thought your concerts was so boisterous! Come

home now and we'll 'ave a party
to celebrate.'

'Most kind, dear lady,' said Mr
String, bowing. He was feeling
quite silly and rather sorry for
the huge wrestlers, who were

very crestfallen.

What a party it was! Everyone came. They all had bubbly champagne and sang and danced merrily late into the night.

Mr String soon forgot his

embarrassment and invited them all to his *real* concert the very next day.

At last, as the stars faded into morning, Mrs Muskett shooed them off home and Mr String to bed.

As he fell asleep, dreaming happily, the silver cup seemed to wink at him.

'Tomorrow,' he thought, 'I shall be famous for my sparkling solos; but tonight, I am Maestro, THE CHAMP!'

Also in Young Puffin

THE GHOST
FAMILY ROBINSON

Martin Waddell

"You know the Robinsons don't like being lonely," I said. "They'd be frightened in your house, all on their own."

The Robinsons are not ghosts who like being left alone. And they don't like not being believed in either, as Tom's parents find out when the Robinsons come to stay.

Also in Young Puffin

DUSTBIN CHARLIE

Ann Pilling

"Is a skip bigger than a dustbin?"
"*Much* bigger."
"Well, they're getting one for
Number 10."

Charlie had always liked seeing what
people threw out in their dustbins. So
he's thrilled to find the toy of his dreams
among the rubbish in the skip. But
during the night, someone else takes it.

Also in Young Puffin

CLASS THREE AND THE BEANSTALK

Martin Waddell

A GIANT beanstalk and a BIG surprise!

Class Three's project on growing things
gets out of hand after they plant a packet
of Jackson's Giant Bean seeds. The
resulting beanstalk keeps growing...and
growing...and growing...
Wilbur Small is coming home! Everyone
is delighted and making great
preparations. All except for the Grice
family who are new and don't know what
all the fuss is about...

Also in Young Puffin

The
Twig Thing

Jan Mark

**As soon as Rosie and Ella saw the
house they knew that something
was missing.**

It has lots of windows and stairs, but
where is the garden? After they move in,
Rosie finds a twig thing which she puts in
water on the window-sill. Gradually
things begin to change.

Also in Young Puffin

Mr Majeika

and the

Haunted Hotel

Humphrey Carpenter

Spooks and spectres at the *Green Banana*!

Class Three of St Barty's are off on an outing to Hadrian's Wall with their teacher, Mr Majeika (who happens to be a magician). Stranded in the fog when the tyres of their coach are mysteriously punctured, they take refuge in a nearby hotel called the Green Banana. Soon some very spooky things start to happen. Strange lights, ghostly sounds and vanishing people...

GEORGE SPEAKS

Dick King-Smith

Laura's baby brother George was four weeks old when it happened.

George looks like an ordinary baby, with his round red face and squashy nose. But Laura soon discovers that he's absolutely *extraordinary*, and everyone's life is turned upside down from the day George speaks!